The Night Walker

To Maggee, who—very generously—lets me borrow her stories
-Richard

This book is dedicated with love to the memory of my mother Joan,
and to Jean Smart, both of whom always supported my art
-Martin

Text copyright © 2002 by Richard Thompson
Illustrations copyright © 2002 by Martin Springett

Published in Canada by Fitzhenry & Whiteside,
195 Allstate Parkway, Markham, Ontario L3R 4T8

Published in the United States, 2003 by Fitzhenry & Whiteside,
121 Harvard Avenue, Suite 2, Allston, Massachusetts 02134

www.fitzhenry.ca   godwit@fitzhenry.ca.

10 9 8 7 6 5 4 3 2 1

Canadian Cataloguing in Publication Data
Thompson, Richard, 1951-
The night walker / by Richard Thompson ; illustration by Martin Springett.

ISBN 1-55041-672-3 (bound).--ISBN 1-55041-784-3 (pbk.)

I. Springett, Martin II. Title.

PS8589.H53N53 2002   jC813'.54   C2002-901605-3
PZ7

U.S. Publisher Cataloging-in-Publication Data
(Library of Congress Standards)

Thompson, Richard.
The night walker / by Richard Thompson ; illustrations by Martin Springet. –1st ed.
[32] p. : col. ill. ;   cm.
Summary: A boy collects objects from the wilderness to take back home. As his pouch fills with treasure,
the boy hears behind him strange sounds that get louder and louder. He wonders if the dreaded Night Walker
has come to snatch him, or has his imagination carried him too far.
ISBN 1-55041-672-3
ISBN 1-55041-784-3 (pbk.)
1. Night -- Fiction. 2. Fear – Fiction. I. Springet, Martin. II. Title.
[E] 21   2002   AC CIP

Fitzhenry & Whiteside acknowledges with thanks the Canada Council for the Arts, the Government of Canada through the
Book Publishing Industry Development Program (BPIDP), and the Ontario Arts Council for their support for our publishing program.

Printed in Hong Kong
Design by Wycliffe Smith Design Inc.

The Night Walker

BY RICHARD THOMPSON

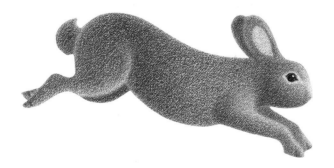

ILLUSTRATED BY MARTIN SPRINGETT

Fitzhenry & Whiteside

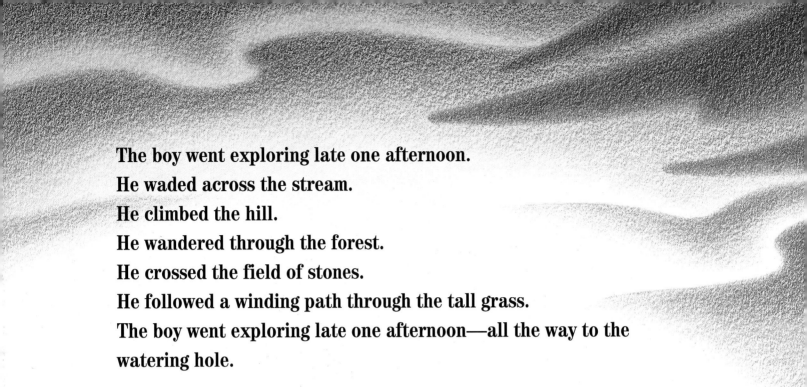

The boy went exploring late one afternoon.

He waded across the stream.

He climbed the hill.

He wandered through the forest.

He crossed the field of stones.

He followed a winding path through the tall grass.

The boy went exploring late one afternoon—all the way to the watering hole.

The boy always carried a knobbly stick for poking into holes, and for helping him balance on steep places, and just in case. And he always carried, tied to his belt, a pouch that he could close by pulling on a string—to collect his treasures in.

On this late afternoon, the boy found a nail and three coins. He put those treasures in his pouch. In the forest he found a smooth, green rock and a small piece of wood that looked like a man running. Amongst the stones in the field of stones, he found a feather that might have been an eagle's feather. Near the watering hole, he found a few dried leaves from a sweet-breath bush. His mother would like those leaves.

The boy was so intent on looking for treasures to put
in his pouch that he didn't notice the sun going down.
And then it was dark, and the boy was a long way from home.

He started back through the tall grass. The night was full of sounds. He could hear an owl calling. He could hear insects churring and whirring. He could hear—and then not quite hear— the sighing song of the night breeze. And then, he realized he could hear something else...

...a clinking sound,
a clicking sound,
a rustling sound...
very close by.

He stopped. He couldn't hear the something else now—
just the owl, and the insects, and the breeze.

He started walking again.

And now he could hear it again…
a clinking sound,
a clicking sound,
a rustling sound.

He stopped. The sound stopped. He walked. He could hear the
sound again.

Something was following him!

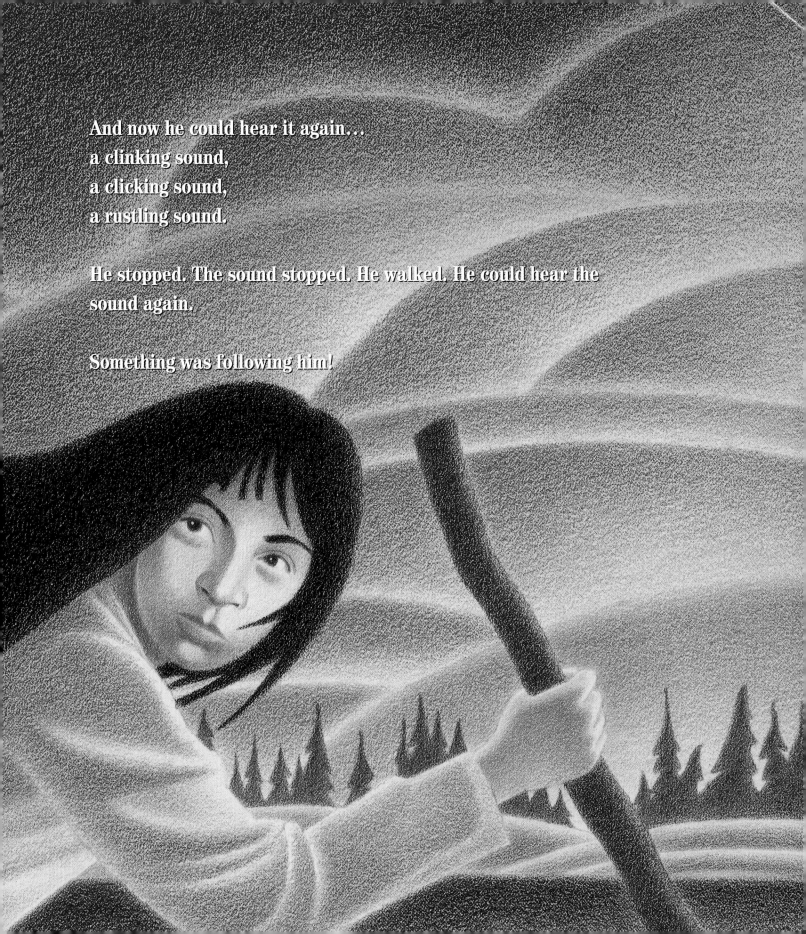

The boy told himself that it was a rabbit moving in the grass.
A rabbit was nothing to be afraid of. But maybe it was something bigger…

Maybe it was a wild dog or a fox. A wild dog
or a fox was nothing to be afraid of. He had his knobbly
stick, just in case, and he could chase away a wild dog
or a fox.

But he walked faster. And whateveritwas walked faster.

It might be a panther. The Boy walked faster again.
And whateveritwas walked faster again.

Or it might be a bear.

Or it might be one of those creatures in the stories that told you to never-go-out-in-the-night-alone—a Night Walker!

A Night Walker had long, sharp claws. And the boy could hear them clicking against the stones on the path!

A Night Walker carried a sack. And the boy could hear the rustling sound of the boy-catching sack dragging along the ground!

A Night Walker had bits of chains around its ankles
because it had been chained in a dark place, and it had
broken loose to wander. The boy could hear the bits of
chain clinking!

A knobbly stick would not scare
a Night Walker.

The boy started to run. And he could hear the Night Walker running right behind him.

He ran faster. And he could hear the Night Walker clinking and clicking and rustling faster behind him.

He could hear the Night Walker's loud breathing! Any moment now, long, sharp claws would reach out of the dark and grab him.

All of a sudden, the boy was tumbling and tumbling.
He had tripped on a stone or a root. His heart clenched
as he waited for the Night Walker to pounce.

But when he stopped tumbling, all he could hear was
the thunder of his blood and the tornado of his breathing.

And, as the storm of his fear blew away, the boy could hear
no sound at all.

For a long time the boy listened.
He listened, and he heard no clinking sound.
He listened, and he heard no clicking sound.
He listened, and he heard no rustling sound.
But, eventually, he heard an owl call. He heard insects churring
and whirring. And maybe the sound of the breeze.

Was the Night Walker gone, or was he standing and listening too? The boy dared not move. He sat very still. And listened.

Eventually, though, the boy grew weary from the hard work of listening…and he fell asleep.

When the sun came up, the boy stood and looked around.

He was in the field of stones at the bottom of the short slope
he had tumbled down in the dark. Nearby lay his knobbly stick.
His pouch had come undone and was lying on the ground.
The boy picked up the stick and the pouch, and started
quickly for home.

Birds were singing, and the boy sang too.

The boy sang as he hurried through the field of stones.
He sang as he hurried through the forest.
He sang as he hurried over the hill and across the stream.
He sang, but he hurried, because he knew that his mother
would be very angry.

But the boy's mother was so happy to see him home and safe that she forgot about being angry.

The boy's mother hugged him, and said, "Tell me your story."

The boy told his story. About how he had wandered
too far, and how the sun had gone down, and how
the whateveritwas had followed him and
changed from a rabbit into a wild dog
and from a wild dog into a panther, and how
the boy had known that it was really
a Night Walker.

He told about how the Night Walker
had chased him, and how
he had fallen.

When the story was finished, the boy showed his mother the treasures he had found.

"A nail and three coins…" They made a soft clinking sound as they tumbled from his hand.

"A smooth, green rock and a piece of wood that looks like a man running…" He laid them down. They made a very small clicking sound.

"And a feather and some dried leaves from a sweet-breath bush. The leaves are for you, Mother." The leaves rustled as he spread them out.

His mother smiled. "You know, my boy," she said, "sometimes the monster you hear behind you in the dark is only the clink and click and rustle of the things you have collected during the day."

"Or it might be the Night Walker,"
said the boy.

"True," said his mother. "It might be
the Night Walker."